Milo

and the Flapjack Fiasco

For the little Apples—Will and Olivia—P.J.

For Jake Paxton, who I'll bet loves flapjacks—M.J.

Text copyright © 2004 by Pamela Jane
Illustrations copyright © 2004 by Meredith Johnson
under exclusive license to MONDO Publishing

For information contact:
MONDO Publishing
980 Avenue of the Americas
New York, NY 10018
Visit our web site at http://www.mondopub.com
Printed in China
04 05 06 07 08 09 HC 9 8 7 6 5 4 3 2 1
04 05 06 07 08 09 PB 9 8 7 6 5 4 3 2 1

ISBN 1-59336-113-0 (hardcover)   ISBN 1-59336-114-9 (pbk.)

Designed by Edward Miller

Library of Congress Cataloging-in-Publication Data

Jane, Pamela.
Milo and the flapjack fiasco / by Pamela Jane ; illustrated by Meredith Johnson.
p. cm.
Summary: Milo tries to help his big sister Sam prepare a flapjack breakfast for her teacher.
ISBN 1-59336-113-0 (hc.) — ISBN 1-59336-114-9 (pbk.)
[1. Pancakes, waffles, etc.—Fiction. 2. Brothers and sisters—Fiction.
3. Teachers—Fiction. 4. Breakfasts—Fiction.] I. Johnson, Meredith, ill. II. Title.

PZ7.J2345Mi 2004   [E]—dc21   2003050999

Milo

and the Flapjack Fiasco

by Pamela Jane

Illustrated by Meredith Johnson

Milo's big sister, Sam, raced into the kitchen.

"Guess what happened at school today?" she cried.

4

Milo plugged his ears. He knew what was coming. All Sam ever talked about was her teacher, Mrs. Bell.

"Mrs. Bell chose me to be line leader!"
Sam would brag. Or "Mrs. Bell let me
be paper passer."

Even Wolf, Milo's dog, was sick of hearing about Mrs. Bell. Wolf howled whenever he heard her name.

Awoooooooo

"Milo, did you hear what I said?
Mrs. Bell is coming over for breakfast
on Saturday!" Sam yelled.
    Milo unplugged his ears.

"I'll make my famous flapjacks,"
Mom said.

Milo's mom called pancakes *flapjacks*,
and no one made them better.

"We'll lock Wolf up so he doesn't mess everything up," added Sam.

Sparkle, Sam's goldfish, flicked her tail as if she agreed.

"Wolf won't mess anything up," said
Milo. "He's a good dog. Wolf, sit!"
Wolf rolled over.

Milo and Sam were setting the table
Saturday morning when Mom walked in.

"Mom, your nose looks funny," said Sam.

"And your eyes are all red," Milo added.

"I feel awful," Mom said. "I think I have a . . . ahh . . . AHH . . . "

"A cold?" Sam guessed.

"Ahh-CHOO!" Mom sneezed and nodded yes. "I have to go back to bed."

"But who will make the flapjacks?"
asked Milo.

"I will!" said Sam. "Milo, fill the water
glasses!"

Sam took out flour and eggs and milk.
She measured and poured and mixed.

"I'm going to make one giant flapjack!" Sam bragged, pouring the batter into the pan. "It will be the best, most fantastic flapjack ever!"

The doorbell rang.

"Milo, flip the flapjack," ordered Sam.
"I'll be back in *one minute*. Make sure
Wolf stays out of trouble!"

"How can Wolf get into trouble in one minute?" asked Milo.

Now Milo had never flipped a flapjack before. He grabbed the frying pan, closed his eyes, and flipped. The giant flapjack went flying over his head and landed right in Wolf's open mouth!

At that moment Sam and Mrs. Bell walked in.

"Something smells good!" said Mrs. Bell. "What's for breakfast?"

Sam smiled proudly. "I've created the best, most fantastic—"

"Glumph!" said Wolf, gulping down the last of the flapjack.

Sam stopped. She stared at Wolf and the empty pan.

"The best, most fantastic—game!" Milo
finished. "It's called Gobble and Guess!

First you close your eyes. Then someone gives you something to eat, and you guess what it is."

"What a great idea!" said Mrs. Bell.

Mrs. Bell went first. "Pickles!" she guessed.
Milo was next. "Popcorn!"

"Dog food?" Sam guessed.

"No—leftover hamburger!" laughed Milo.

Milo, Sam, and Mrs. Bell gobbled and guessed and guessed and gobbled all morning.

"Chocolate chips!"

"Peanut butter!"

"Gummy worms!"

"What a wonderful breakfast treat!" said
Mrs. Bell.

"Guess what?" Sam said to her teacher.
"I made the best, most fantastic flapjack
for breakfast, but Wolf ate it."

"He didn't mean to," said Milo. "It just fell into his mouth."

"Milo just thought up the game," Sam explained, "so you wouldn't guess what a big mess he made of things."

"Milo, you are so creative!" said
Mrs. Bell. "I am going to make sure you
are in my class next year."

"With you as my student, it will be the best, most fantastic class ever!"